P9-CTA-234

A Richard Jackson Book

"Are There Any Questions?"

by DENYS CAZET

FALMOUTH PUBLIC LIBRARY

ORCHARD BOOKS • NEW YORK

JJ.
Cazet
MAIN

Also by the author

A Fish in His Pocket
Great-uncle Felix
Mother Night
"Never Spit on Your Shoes"
Daydreams
"I'm Not Sleepy"

Copyright © 1992 by Denys Cazet
All rights reserved. No part of this book may be reproduced or
transmitted in any form or by any means, electronic or mechanical,
including photocopying, recording, or by any information storage or
retrieval system, without permission in writing from the Publisher.

Orchard Books
95 Madison Avenue, New York, NY 10016

Manufactured in the United States of America. Printed by Barton Press, Inc.
Bound by Horowitz/Rae. Book design by Mina Greenstein.
The text of this book is set in 16 point ITC Bookman Light.
The illustrations are watercolor paintings, reproduced in halftone.

10 9 8 7 6 5 4 3 2 1

Library of Congress Cataloging-in-Publication Data
Cazet, Denys.
Are there any questions? / by Denys Cazet.   p.   cm.
"A Richard Jackson book"—Half t.p. Summary: As Mother listens, Arnie,
a first grader, describes his class trip to the aquarium.
ISBN 0-531-05451-9.   ISBN 0-531-08601-1 (lib. bdg.)
[1. Aquariums, Public—Fiction.   2. Mothers and sons—Fiction.]
I. Title. PZ7.C2985Ar 1992 [E]—dc20 91-42977

CHILDREN'S DEPARTMENT
Falmouth Public Library
Falmouth, Mass. 02540

For my grandson,
TY

G-177 708/14 95

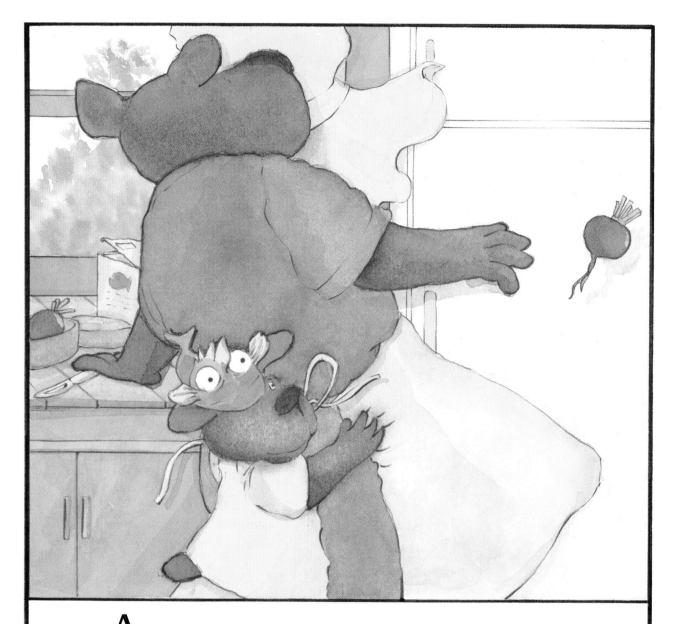

Arnie closed the screen door softly and
tiptoed into the kitchen. He slipped up behind
his mother and threw his arms around her.

"*Oh!*" she shouted.

"*Squid!*" shouted Arnie. "The deadly squid can
squeeze a whale juiceless!"

"I'm not *that* big," said Mother.

She opened the refrigerator. "Tomato juice?"

"Milk, please," said Arnie.

"I love your new hat," said Mother. "Did you get it on the field trip?"

"The aquarium," said Arnie. "First grade only!"

Mother nodded and poured a glass of milk. "Well?" she said. "Tell me all about it!"

. . . name on your lunch and go to the bathroom.

"You have to put your name on your lunch," said Arnie, "go to the bathroom, and hand in your permission slip."

"That's a lot to remember," said Mother.

Arnie shrugged. "Some kids forgot."

But, I don't have to go.

I do, Helen.

Thanks, Arnie.

"The teacher let us choose a buddy," Arnie continued. "I picked Raymond, and Raymond picked me."

Where are you going?

I'm taking Cleo to visit her mother.

Mother opened a box of fish-shaped crackers and poured them into a bowl.

"Goldfish?" she asked.

"Goldfish come from China," said Arnie.

"These come from Shop-N-Save," said Mother.

You . . . will be my partner.

¿?

"I learned a new song on the bus," Arnie said. "I learned to count backward from one hundred!"

"My goodness," said Mother as she scooped up a handful of crackers.

"The balloon fish can eat a hundred times its own weight!" said Arnie. "Every day!"

Mother put the crackers back.

Tweeeet!

. . . goo, gooo, ooou, ahhh, goo, goo, ga, ga . . .

?

. . . ninety-nine bottles of pop on the wall, ninety-nine bottles of pop, if one of those bottles should happen to fall, ninety-eight bottles of pop on the wall; ninety-eight bottles of pop on the wall, ninety-eight bottles of pop, if one of those bottles should happen to fall, ninety-seven bottles of pop on the wall;
AQUARIUM
53
53
Driver! Take these children back to school and put their noses to the grindstone.
Now I remember. Left on 96th.

"When we got to the aquarium, a lady met us at the front door," Arnie said. "She told us all about it."

"Was she a docent?" asked Mother.

"No, I think she was someone's grandma. She showed us all around."

OH!

Look out!

HELP!

Here, kitty, kitty, kitty.

STOP!

Where IS Carmelo Ramirez?

"We saw the crocodiles and the alligators first," said Arnie. "And then, some snakes and big spiders."

"How big?" Mother asked.

"Real big," said Arnie.

"We went into a room where the fishes went around and around and around and around and around," said Arnie. "My eyes got wobbly. I didn't feel so good."

Mother poured some more milk. "And now?"

"Okay," said Arnie. "Better than Raymond. He threw up."

?

Now what?

Busy?

"That's Raymond all over," said Mother. Arnie opened the refrigerator, and Mother took out some salmon croquettes. "Then what?"

"Then we went to the tide pool room," said Arnie. "The lady said we could touch anything we wanted."

"Did you?"

"Almost," Arnie said. "The starfish has suction cups on its feet. It can stick to your face."

Yum.

Brass is better.

Feeding time in the aquarium, boys and girls, a very special time . . .

"We watched them feed the dolphins," said Arnie. "I wanted to see them feed a giant squid. They have beaks and squeeze the living juice—"

"Out of you!" interrupted Mother. "Then what?"

"I guess they eat you," said Arnie.

Mother smiled. "What happened after the dolphins?"

"Oh," said Arnie. "Lunch."

No squids.

Something's broken.

We can fix it. I'll show you.

"After lunch, the lady asked us if we had any questions," Arnie said.

Mother put dinner in the oven. "Did you?"

"I think so," he said.

Here are your hats, boys and girls, and thank you. Are there any questions?

Yeah. How old are you?

Thank you.

Are you kids still on that dang bus?

Mother handed Arnie the dinner dishes. "Did you learn to count forward on the way home?" she asked.

"I can't remember," Arnie said. "It was very quiet."

Arnie's mother ran her fingers through his hair. "I'm glad you had a good day," she said.
"I did!" said Arnie. "I think the teacher did, too. She went home early."

Arnie picked up his hat. "I have to call Raymond," he said. "We have to plan our costume."

"Costume?" Mother said. "Why do you need a costume?"

"For the Halloween parade," Arnie said.

"Don't tell me," said Mother. "You and Raymond are going to be—"

Arnie threw his arms around his mother. "The deadly squid!" he said.

"Thank you," said Mother, "for not using the whale word."